Dayshaun's
Gift

Zetta Elliott

Dayshaun's Gift

Illustrated by Alex Portal

Rosetta
&
Press

Books by Zetta Elliott

A Wave Came Through Our Window
A Wish After Midnight
An Angel for Mariqua
Bird
Fox & Crow: a Christmas Tale
I Love Snow!
Max Loves Muñecas!
Room In My Heart
Ship of Souls
The Boy in the Bubble
The Deep
The Girl Who Swallowed the Sun
The Last Bunny in Brooklyn
The Magic Mirror
The Phoenix on Barkley Street

1

"For the last time, Dayshaun, turn off that TV! Hurry up—we're going to be late."

I blast one more bloodthirsty zombie before pausing the game and putting the controller down. I can tell from the tone of her voice that Mom isn't going to let me stay home and play video games while she goes to the new community garden. Mom volunteers there once a week and that usually means that I have to volunteer, too.

Mom tosses a pair of gardening gloves at me. "You need to get some fresh air and learn how to care for *living* things, Dayshaun. How will you survive the zombie apocalypse if you don't know how to grow your own food?"

I crack a smile even though I'm not happy about gardening on a Saturday morning. Mom's right—the food supply will be seriously disrupted if zombies take over. Once you reach level four of this game, you get to raid grocery stores and abandoned houses for canned goods. We don't have any zombies in our 'hood, but we also don't have a whole lot of grocery stores and the food there isn't all that fresh. Mom and her friends want to start a farmer's market so that people in our community can buy organic vegetables.

Mom smiles at me in the mirror as she ties a scarf over her locks. "You come from a long line of gardeners, Dayshaun. We don't just have green thumbs, we've got soil in our blood. Your grandfather was a wonderful gardener, you know."

Of course, I know. Mom talks about Grandpa *all* the time. I don't really remember my grandfather. He lived in Louisiana and passed away when I was four. Mom misses him a lot. I think she loves gardening because it reminds her of being down South with her dad. I don't think spending hours in the dirt on my hands and knees is much fun. I'm more into *eating* food. Growing it from scratch? Not so much.

When I spend the weekend with my dad, we sleep in, make pancakes, and then watch cartoons until noon. But I spent last weekend with my father, so that means I'm stuck gardening with my mom this weekend. I was pretty mad when my parents got divorced, but I guess I'm used to it now. One good thing about the split is that now my dad buys me lots of stuff. I already know how much he loves me, but I don't say no when Dad offers to buy me new kicks or the latest zombie video game!

I look out the window and see a bright July sun burning in the cloudless, blue Brooklyn sky. Mom reads my mind and snatches something off the coat rack by the front door.

"Here—take your grandfather's old hat to keep the sun off your head," she says.

I take the raggedy old hat and make sure Mom doesn't see me frown. My grandfather's hat looks pretty grubby, and it smells like seventy-five years of sweat. I fold it in half and shove the hat in my back pocket before following Mom out the front door.

Weeksville Heritage Center is just a few blocks away from our apartment building. Most community gardens start out as abandoned lots that neighbors take over and convert into green space. That's what my friends Carlos and Tariq did when a building on their block burned down. But the garden at Weeksville is different. As Mom likes to remind me, Black people have been growing food on this land for almost two hundred years.

Once upon a time, Brooklyn wasn't one of New York City's five boroughs, and there was no bridge connecting it to Manhattan. Brooklyn used to be one of the biggest cities in the country, and it was home to a community of free African Americans called Weeksville. In 1838 James Weeks bought lots of land in Brooklyn, and that's how the community got its name.

I know all this because I attend the Weeksville School. It's in Crown Heights now but it used to be in Weeksville. Back then it was called Colored School #2. Every year my class takes a trip to the Heritage Center for a tour of the three Hunterfly Road houses that are over a hundred years old. Hunterfly Road used to wind through Weeksville before Brooklyn's streets were laid out in a grid.

My teacher says we should care about Weeksville because back in 1970, kids from our school raised almost a thousand dollars to help fix up the old, rundown houses. They also joined the dig that uncovered artifacts from the 1800s. They found marbles and medicine bottles that belonged to people who lived in another century. I think archaeology is pretty cool…but so is blasting zombies!

When Mom stops to talk to our neighbor outside the center, I peek through the fence to see if any other kids have been dragged out of the house on a Saturday morning. Carlos won't be there because he's at robotics camp in Queens, and Tariq is spending the summer with his sister at a sleep away camp upstate. Carlos and Tariq are the only friends I have who are into gardening, and that's because they discovered a magic phoenix was living in the garden on their block. But nothing magical ever happens here at Weeksville.

Through the center's fence I can only see adults in the garden area, and most of them have grey or white hair. I smother a sigh and follow Mom around the corner to the entrance.

2.

It's nice and cool inside the air-conditioned center. A few kids are standing with their parents, but I can tell from the smiles on their faces that they're not here for hard labor. They're probably just here for an art workshop or to see a dance performance. There's always something happening at the center. Ever since this new building opened last year, Mom and I have been coming here a lot to see plays or art exhibits or movies.

My Mom loves this place, but with everything I've already learned at school, I've had just about enough of Weeksville. I like learning about history, but we can't live in the past. That's what my dad always says. Last month I asked him if he and Mom were going to get back together. Dad put his arm around me and said, "We have to live in the here and now, Dayshaun." Sometimes I wish things could be like they were before, but Dad's right. We can't go backward, only forward.

Mom and I leave the air conditioning behind and head outside. The garden is out back, behind the historic houses and their fake privy (that's another word for outhouse). Between the new building and the old ones there's a mini meadow. It's meant to show visitors what the land looked like back in the day, but I think it looks like somebody just couldn't bother to cut the grass!

On the other side of the fence are the low, brick buildings of the Kingsborough housing project. The Weeksville Gardens projects are a few blocks away, right across from my school.

When we reach the garden, all the old-timers stop what they're doing to wave at or hug my mother. I was here just a couple of weeks ago, but they still talk about how fast I'm growing. Then they start talking about the "heirloom seeds" they're going to plant today. An heirloom is something valuable you pass down from generation to generation, but I don't think I'd want to inherit a bunch of seeds—not unless they were magic, like in that fairy tale about Jack and the beanstalk. But Mom and her friends love the idea of growing food that their ancestors used to eat when they were slaves and even way back in Africa. I'd rather have a burger and fries!

I slip away from Mom and the granny gardeners, pull on my gloves, and pick a row where I can work by myself. I like cabbages because it's not hard to tell the difference between a head of cabbage and a weed. With other vegetables I'm not so sure, which means I have to stop and ask someone and *that* always turns into an on-the-spot botany lesson.

Mom doesn't let me bring anything electronic to the garden so there's nothing to distract me. I try to tune out the chatty olds folks and just focus on the weeds. I yank them out, one by one, while wishing a giant would come along and yank *me* out of this garden.

Before long the brutal sun overhead has me sweating like a pig. I don't want to wear my grandfather's smelly old hat, but I don't want to get sunstroke either. I reach back and pull the scruffy hat out of my pocket. I look around to make sure no one I know can see me before putting the hat on my head.

Grandpa must have had a real big head because his hat almost covers my eyes. I push it back a bit so I can see, and suddenly it feels like I've just put on a pair of sunglasses. Everything around me takes on a strange orange glow but within seconds, the bright orange tint fades to brown. Then everything that was green turns grey. I feel like I'm in one of those old black and white movies that my mother loves to watch.

I rub my eyes but that only makes things worse because suddenly the garden starts to spin! I crouch down and grab hold of the only thing I can see clearly—a head of cabbage. My breakfast feels like it wants to leave my belly, so I press my eyes and lips shut. When I open them again, the spinning has stopped and everything in the garden is green once more.

3.

I look around for my mom but all the grown-ups have disappeared. I'm alone in the garden except for a small rabbit that's standing up on its haunches, watching me. I've never seen a rabbit in the garden before, and so I reach out my hand to see if I can coax her a little bit closer. Then a woman's sharp voice calls out, "You—boy! Get out of my vegetable patch!"

I look up and see a scowling woman with a

broom in her hand standing on the back steps of the 1860s house. "Get your hands off my cabbage!" she hollers with a menacing shake of her broom.

I let go of the cabbage and slowly pull myself to my feet. This woman in a long dress is the only adult I can see. Where's my mom? I look down and realize I'm no longer standing in the back row of the big community garden. How did I wind up in some stranger's backyard?

"Sorry, ma'am," I say as I carefully step around the neatly planted vegetables in her "patch."

For a moment I stand frozen, unsure what to do. White sheets pinned to a clothesline flap in the breeze. Then the door to a nearby privy opens and that same breeze fills my nostrils with a nasty smell. An older man tucks his shirt into his pants and pulls up his suspenders. "Can I help you, son?" he asks in a kind voice.

My mom always told me to find an elder if I ever needed help when she wasn't around. I *think* I need help—I mean, I am definitely lost. But something about the old-fashioned clothes these Black folks are wearing stops me from hanging around. Plus they're looking at *me* like I might be an alien. So I just force myself to smile and wave before following the dirt path that seems to lead to the front of the house.

I don't know where I am, but I am definitely *not* at the Weeksville Heritage Center any more. The first thing I notice is that only one wooden house is standing where four houses used to be—five, really, because the 1860s house is a duplex (two houses joined together). Instead of a mini meadow there's long grass and wildflowers everywhere—and the center's new building is gone!

I'm standing by a dirt road. I've never seen a dirt road in Brooklyn before. My eyes still feel a bit fuzzy, but it looks like someone is coming up the road—on a horse! Chickens cluck inside of the fenced yard behind me and I can see a cow grazing in a field. There are more wooden houses farther down the road. Each house seems to have its own garden and outhouse.

Suddenly I hear a boy's voice call out, "I did it—I win!"

I walk up the road a bit to where a couple of kids are kneeling on the ground in front of a small house. A circle has been drawn in the dirt and it looks like the two boys have just finished playing a game of marbles.

"Who are you?" asks a boy who looks like he might be about my age.

"I'm Dayshaun," I say with an awkward smile.
I try not to look as nervous as I feel with the boys'

eyes sweeping over me from head to toe.

The older boy narrows his eyes and sizes me up. "You're not from Weeksville, are you? Don't think I've seen you around."

"I—I'm just visiting," I stammer and quickly follow up with a question of my own. "What's your name?"

"I'm Teddy and this sore loser is Frankie. Funny hat you got there. Where'd you get it?" he asks.

I can't tell if the gleam in Teddy's eyes is just curiosity or suspicion.

I take my grandfather's hat off and shove it in my back pocket. "Uh—it was a gift. What street is this?" I ask.

"This is Hunterfly Road," he replies.

Hunterfly Road? THE Hunterfly Road that used to run through Weeksville back in the day? My heart starts to race as I consider the possibilities. Maybe I have sunstroke. Maybe I passed out and this is just a dream. Or maybe—just maybe—I've traveled back in time! Everything around me looks like it belongs in the past—including this boy. But he'll think I'm nuts if I tell him I'm from the future.

"What'd you say your name was?" I ask with a friendly smile.

The boy puffs out his chest and shows me a handful of gleaming glass marbles. "I'm Teddy Gaines, Marbles Champion of the World!" he says proudly.

Frankie sulks and puts his hands on his hips. "You can't be the best in the world when you've never even left Brooklyn."

Teddy frowns and thinks about that for a moment. Then he says, "Well…I'm still the best player around these parts. Now hand over that green marble, Frankie. I won it fair and square."

Just then an older girl comes out of the house. She looks like a teenager but she's dressed just like the lady with the broom. The girl opens the gate that separates the yard from the road and says, "Teddy Gaines, you better not take anything away from that child. His mother's feeling poorly and here you are robbing him of his only toy."

Teddy looks genuinely hurt. "I ain't robbing nobody! I knocked his marble clean out the circle. The rules say it's mine now, Susan Smith."

The girl tucks a stray curl behind her ear and hoists a heavy wicker basket farther up her arm. "Well, *I* say it isn't. I just gave Mrs. Wilson some chamomile tea to help her sleep. You take his last marble and that boy will start hollering, which will set the baby to crying, which will prevent Mrs.

Wilson from getting any rest. Is that what you want?"

Teddy kicks at the dusty ground but says nothing to the older girl. Frankie sticks his tongue out at Teddy and quickly scampers inside the house still clutching his prize marble.

4.

Teddy turns to me. "You want to play?"

I shake my head and show him my empty hands. "I don't have any marbles." I've never played marbles, either, but I figure Teddy doesn't need to know that right now. And there's no point telling him how good I am at blasting zombies!

"You from Manhattan?" he asks.

"Crown Heights," I say.

"You mean Crow Hill?" asks the older girl.

"We're heading out that way."

"We are?" Teddy looks at her like he has other plans.

"*Yes*, we are," the girl replies firmly. "I can't carry this basket of food out there by myself. And it's not like you have anything better to do." She turns to me and smiles. "I'm Susan Smith."

Something about this girl makes me feel like I should bow or offer to shake her hand. Instead I just smile back and shyly say, "I'm Dayshaun Arnold."

"Well, Dayshaun, you can come with us if you want. 'Many hands make light work.'"

I don't know what else to do with myself so I just nod and reach for the heavy basket Susan's holding. Teddy tries to grab it first and for a moment we play tug of war, which makes Susan roll her eyes.

She swats our hands away and says, "Why don't you each take one handle and carry it between you?"

Susan sets the basket on the ground and heads down the dusty road. Teddy and I look at each other and then do just what Susan suggested. With the basket swinging between us, we hurry to catch up with her.

My stomach growls and I wonder just what kind of food is under the checkered cloth that covers the basket. I glance at my watch but it's frozen at 9:52am. It must be lunchtime by now.

"Who's all this food for?" I ask.

Teddy and Susan both give me a funny look. I feel my cheeks burn and wonder if I've said something wrong.

"Didn't you hear about the riots over in Manhattan?" Susan asks. "They started on

Monday."

Riots? Mom and I watch the news together every evening. I know there has been trouble in Ferguson, Missouri and Baltimore, Maryland, but I haven't heard about any riots in New York City.

Mom says people who feel they have no power need some way to make their voices heard. Sometimes that means marching in the street, and sometimes that means smashing things and setting fires. Mom says it's best to protest peacefully, but to always remember that people matter more than things. You can replace a broken window but you can't bring somebody back to life.

"If you want peace, listen." That's what my dad always says. I'm new to this world, and I definitely don't want to run into any trouble while I'm here. I decide to learn as much as I can from Teddy and Susan about the riots.

"Was anybody hurt?" I ask.

Teddy whistles and solemnly shakes his head. "Plenty of colored folks have been attacked and it ain't over yet. The mob even burned down the Colored Orphan Asylum."

"Mob?"

Susan sighs impatiently. "You're confusing him, Teddy! Start at the beginning."

"I did!" Teddy complains. "On *Monday* the rioters went after the orphans."

"You have to tell him *why* that happened, not *when*," says Susan.

Teddy just rolls his eyes so Susan takes over and tells me the story herself. "President Lincoln needs more soldiers to win the war, so he started the draft."

I nod and pretend I understand but in my mind I'm thinking, *soldiers*? If Abraham Lincoln is president right now, then Susan must be talking about the Civil War. I try to remember when the Civil War took place. My Social Studies teacher had a special word for the anniversary of the end of the war—*sesquicentennial*—but I can't remember just how many years have passed. What I do know is, I really am in a whole other century!

Susan thinks I understand her and so she keeps going. "A lot of poor white men got drafted into the Union Army, but rich white men could buy their way out for $300. The poor men felt that was unfair, and so they set fire to the draft office. Things just got out of control after that. The mob started attacking every Negro in sight, and there was nothing the police could do. So colored people fled to Weeksville where they knew they'd be safe. Some of them have been camping in the woods since Monday. It's Thursday now and they just keep coming."

It takes a moment for me to realize that my mouth is hanging open. I can't believe this happened—*is happening now*—right here in New York City. We don't use words like "Negro" or "colored" any more, but I know Susan is talking about people like us—African Americans.

"Why are they mad at *us*?" I finally ask.

Teddy spits into the dirt at our feet. "White folks are always mad at us."

Susan shakes her head. "That's not true—not all of them. There are plenty of white abolitionists who hate slavery."

"That don't mean they love us!" Teddy exclaims. He turns back to me. "The rioters blame us for the war and they don't want slavery to end."

If Susan doesn't become a doctor, she'll make a real good teacher. I listen as she schools Teddy.

"Try to see it from their point of view. Many of the rioters are poor Irish immigrants. They think freed slaves will flood into the North and take all the jobs. It's competition they fear, not Negroes. That's why they attacked the colored workers in the tobacco factory last summer over in Cobble Hill. Plus no one wants to be sent off to war."

"I do! I ain't afraid to fight," cries Teddy. "They

ought to let colored men here in New York enlist in the army. I'd show those Rebs a thing or two."

"You're just a boy, Teddy, not a soldier," says Susan.

"Well, you're just a girl! If *you* can become a doctor, then *I* can become a soldier—or a general, even!"

I stop their bickering by asking another question. "So if the police can't stop the rioters, what can kids like us do to help?"

Susan nods at the basket, which is becoming heavier now that the road is heading up a steep hill. "Just what we're doing right now. My mother gave us some food to share with the survivors."

"And we took them blankets and some extra clothes yesterday," Teddy adds.

Susan pats a leather satchel that hangs at her side. "I also brought some bandages in case there are wounds that need tending."

Teddy nudges me with his elbow and sneers, "Susan's always looking for a chance to play nurse."

Susan keeps her eyes on the road ahead. "Only children play games, Teddy. I'm practicing medicine."

"Ha! I wouldn't let you practice on me!" Teddy says with disdain. "Pa says girls can't be doctors. They ain't got the right temperament."

Susan flashes her angry eyes at Teddy. "I'm cleverer than most boys, I'm not faint-hearted, and I have a steady hand. Why shouldn't I go to medical school?"

"If you go to medical school, you'll take the place of a boy who actually deserves to be there," Teddy says with a mischievous gleam in his eye.

"I will not!" Susan insists. "My mother told me a lady doctor is taking steps right now to open a medical college for women here in New York."

Teddy looks disappointed to hear this, but he still comes up with a way to irritate Susan. He smirks and says, "A *white* lady doctor, right? You think she's going to let a colored girl like *you* go to *her* school?"

I decide I better jump in before Susan loses her cool. "Where I'm from," I say, "girls can do just about anything boys can do. They're police officers, soldiers, lawyers—and doctors. We may even have a woman president someday."

Teddy laughs out loud, but I keep going. "Telling Susan she can't go to medical school because she's a girl is like white folks telling you what you can and can't do because you're—" I almost say "Black" but catch myself in time. "Because you're colored."

Teddy thinks about that for a moment. Then

he says, "Well, she's got two strikes against her then because she's colored *and* a girl."

Now it's my turn to laugh. "I'm sure that won't stop Susan. She'll just have to work twice as hard."

"Thank you, Dayshaun. That's just what I plan to do," Susan says. Then she beams at me and I feel my cheeks burn again.

Teddy squints at me. "Where'd you say you were from?"

Before I can answer, Teddy trips on a rock and nearly sends us tumbling back down the hill. Susan quickly reaches out a hand to steady him. Teddy quietly thanks her and forgets about interrogating me.

5.

We don't say much until we reach the top of the hill. I ask if we can stop to catch our breath, and Susan suggests we set the heavy basket down. Teddy and I use the back of our hands to wipe away the sweat running down our faces. Susan pulls a frilly handkerchief from inside her long sleeve and daintily dabs at her brow.

I'm the only one wearing shorts and a t-shirt. Susan has on a long dress and Teddy's wearing pants and a shirt with the sleeves rolled up. If I was in *my* Brooklyn, I'd take my t-shirt off but I get the feeling kids don't do that here.

"It sure is hot today," Teddy says with a resentful glance at the sun overhead. "I hope it cools down soon."

Susan nods and fans herself with her hankie. "People drink more when it's hot and then they loiter in the street looking for trouble. A day of rain would help put out the fires, and it might send the rioters back home where they belong," she says.

I think about the rioters in Manhattan. After days of destroying the city, are they still angry or just drunk and bored? Then I think about how hectic things can get in my neighborhood sometimes when there's a heat wave. When the temperatures rise, some people just seem to lose their minds.

"My Pa says the mayor's called up the soldiers from Gettysburg," Teddy says hopefully. "They'll teach those rioters a thing or two!"

Susan sighs heavily and tucks her kerchief back into her sleeve. "And then they'll march off to war—again. I pray for peace every night," she says wearily, "but sometimes I fear this war will never end."

I want to tell Susan not to worry. I want to reassure her that the Civil War will end, the North will win, and slavery will be abolished. Mom and I celebrated Juneteenth just last month—at Weeksville, of course. But if I tell Susan what I know, Teddy will ask me more questions that I won't be able to answer without admitting that I'm from the future. So instead I just ask, "How much farther do we have to go?"

Susan points to a wooded area in the valley below. "That's where we're headed," she says.

The forest isn't big or dense, and I can see people moving between the trees. I've gone camping with my dad before, but I can't imagine living in the woods without a tent or sleeping bag because a mob chased me away from my home.

"Be gentle with them," Susan says in a soft voice. "They've been through a terrible ordeal. Many have lost their homes and some have lost family members as well." She pauses to take a deep breath and then leads us down the hill and into the woods.

It's dim and cool beneath the trees, but no one here looks very comfortable. These folks have had to sleep on the ground, and most look like they're wearing the same clothes they had on when they fled Manhattan.

Walking into the camp of survivors made me think about the pictures my teacher showed our class of people who survived the attack on 9/11. When the trains stopped running, people had to walk across the Brooklyn Bridge to get home. Some were covered in white dust—or blood. Most people looked frightened but others just looked numb, like they didn't know *what* to feel.

The people huddled in the woods have that same look. I can tell these folks have been through a lot.

I'm not sure what to say or do, and I think Teddy feels the same. We stand awkwardly in the clearing waiting for Susan to give us instructions.

"Set the basket down over there," she says, pointing to a flat tree stump that can serve as a sort of table.

We do as we're told and watch as several women cautiously step forward to inspect the contents of the basket. They remove all the food and then divide it up so that everyone gets something to eat.

I see that at least one small fire has been built, and whatever's cooking in that cast iron pot smells pretty good. I think about the rabbit I saw earlier this morning and figure maybe the fresh vegetables we brought can be added to the stew. My stomach rumbles but I don't have time to worry about myself. All I want to do right now is help the folks huddled here in the woods.

"Good afternoon. How are you feeling today?"

Susan greets everyone she sees with a warm smile. I watch as she moves from person to person, squeezing an elderly man's sunken shoulder, caressing a little girl's tear-stained cheek. An old woman who is laid out on the ground on a tattered quilt grasps Susan's hand and says, "God bless you, child."

Susan blinks back tears and squeezes the old woman's hand for a long moment before moving on to a little boy with a bloody bandage wrapped around his head.

"Let's take a look at that scratch," Susan says in a cheerful voice. The boy nods silently and sits without fidgeting as Susan unwinds the bandage.

I step closer and see that what Susan called a scratch is actually a pretty deep wound. "What happened to him?" I ask quietly. The boy looks at me but lets Susan do all the talking.

"The rioters chased him and his family out of their home. His neighbor told me they were throwing bricks and bottles—whatever they could get their hands on. A paving stone glanced off his head."

I'm just a few years older than this boy, but I'd be crying my eyes out if I were in his position. It's only been an hour since I traveled through time and I'm a little homesick already. The boy's silence seems strange to me, but Susan said to be gentle so I take a seat beside him on the mossy log.

"I'm Dayshaun. What's your name?"

The boy kicks his heels against the log but doesn't answer me. I try again. "Where's your

43

mom and dad?"

Susan quickly shakes her head, silently warning me to stop. It takes me a few seconds to figure it out. Attacked, injured, *and* separated from his parents? This kid's been through a lot. I search for something safe to say. "You can squeeze my hand if it hurts," I offer.

The boy doesn't look at me, but he does nod. Then he wraps his little fingers around mine and sits as still as a statue while Susan ties a fresh bandage over the wound on his head.

I scan the camp for Teddy and find him talking to an elderly man who is sitting on a large rock. He's wearing just one shoe because his other foot is bandaged and propped up on an empty wooden crate. Susan finishes binding the boy's head and nods in Teddy's direction.

"That's Mr. Williams," she says. "We had to cut

his shoe off. Once the swelling goes down, we'll find him a new pair."

I watch as Teddy searches the forest floor for a sturdy branch. When he finds one he likes, he pulls a small knife from his pocket and starts stripping the branch of leaves and twigs.

"What's Teddy doing?" I ask Susan.

"Why don't you go over there and find out?" she replies. Susan pulls a square of brown paper from her skirt pocket, unfolds it, and offers the boy a peppermint. He immediately lets go of my hand and reaches for the candy. A huge smile lights up his face as he pops the sweet treat into his mouth.

That's when I realize that Teddy couldn't be more wrong. Susan will make a great doctor someday.

6.

I get up from the log and go over to Teddy. Before I can ask him what he's doing, Teddy hands me the branch and starts looking for another. Mr. Williams chuckles and says to me, "Your friend's got a plan to get me back on my feet."

I smile but in my mind I'm thinking that this old man really shouldn't *be* on his feet. With his long white beard and stooped shoulders, Mr. Williams looks like he belongs in a rocking chair—or a nursing home.

For the first time today, Teddy isn't playing around. I'm surprised but also impressed by how he's helping a total stranger.

"What's your plan?" I ask Teddy.

"Mr. Williams needs a crutch so he can get around. This stick should work," he says confidently.

"Just one?" I ask. "One stick is a cane. For a crutch you need two sticks tied together."

Teddy looks confused so I pick up a twig and try to draw a diagram in the soft dirt on the forest floor. I twisted my ankle playing soccer last year so I draw my crutches from memory.

"You want to make two crutches with four sticks?" Teddy asks. He looks skeptical and so does Mr. Williams.

"You can move a lot faster with two crutches," I explain, "because you sort of swing along."

Teddy still looks uncertain so I agree to make just one crutch using two sticks. That's probably a better idea since we don't even have any tools.

"I'm going to look over there for another stick," Teddy says. "Wait here."

I watch as Teddy picks his way through the woods, carefully stepping around families that have set up lean-tos or laid pallets on the ground. I clutch the stick Teddy gave me and try to think of something to say to Mr. Williams. He looks pretty frail to me. Even if Teddy does make him a crutch, where exactly is he going to go?

The old man seems to read my mind. He winks at me and says, "Don't know where I'll be heading next, but the good Lord brung me this far. I figure I better be ready to keep on going till I can't go no more. Once the war is over I'll see which way the wind is blowing. I always did want to see Africa.

Maybe I'll rest my weary bones over in Liberia. My granny was African, you know."

Mr. Williams sounds a bit like my relatives from Louisiana. "Where are you from, sir?" I ask.

"Born and raised in Virginny," he says with another smile. "Caught that freedom train and reached New York when I was just a young man. Been here ever since. The folks I traveled with kept on going up to Canada—they were afraid slave catchers would find them in the city. But soon as I stepped off that ship, I knew I'd found my promised land."

I want to ask Mr. Williams whether he took a ship or a train—or both—but old folks get confused sometimes, so I just leave it alone. I also want to ask him why he's so determined to stay in such a dangerous place. If slave catchers found him, he could have been taken back to Virginia as a slave. And now the rioters in Manhattan have left him hurt and homeless.

I don't think I'd go back to a neighborhood where I knew I wasn't wanted. In *my* Brooklyn, whites and Blacks don't mix all that much. There aren't any white kids in my school, though my mom says gentrification is going to change that. She says it's good for different kinds of people to mix together so long as everyone is treated with respect and the neighborhood's history is preserved. I just want to live somewhere safe. When you're at home you should feel like you're wanted—like you belong.

Mr. Williams groans softly as he reaches down to rub his swollen ankle. "You must think I'm crazy to stay, huh? Well, I guess I am kind of stubborn. But this ain't the first riot I've lived through, son, and it probably won't be the last. They tried to run us out of town back in '34—even burned our church to the ground. But we rebuilt then and we'll do it again once things cool down a bit."

If a group of people told me I couldn't live in Brooklyn any more, would I pack up and leave or stand my ground? Mr. Williams looks old and frail, but he's actually a pretty tough dude. "I don't think you're crazy," I tell him. Then I add, "I think you're really brave." I hope he knows I mean it.

For just a moment I think about my grandfather and wonder what stories he might have told me if he'd lived a few more years. I reach back and touch the hat stuffed in my pocket. This journey started when I put on Grandpa's hat. Maybe this is his way of telling me a story.

Just then Teddy comes back with another sturdy stick in one hand and a small hatchet in the other.

"Will this do?" he asks me.

I nod and we put the two sticks side by side on the ground. One is longer than the other so Teddy swings the hatchet and cuts it down to size.

"What do we do next?" he asks.

I look at the diagram I drew in the dirt. Then I move the tops of the sticks about six inches apart.

"We'll need two shorter sticks here and here," I explain to Teddy. "One will go under his arm and he can hold onto the other one with his hand."

While Teddy's looking around for the short sticks, I use the hatchet to cut the bottom of one stick at an angle. Now the two long sticks form a perfect triangle. Teddy comes back and puts the two short sticks in place. We stand back and look at our crutch with satisfaction.

"All we need now is a way to hold it all together," I say.

"My Pa has lots of tools," says Teddy, "but it'll take me a while to run home and get them."

"We got everything we need right here," says Mr. Williams. "There are nails in this old crate. I'm sure you boys are strong enough to pull it apart."

Teddy and I carefully lift Mr. Williams'
bandaged foot off the crate and set it down on
the ground. Then we do our best to pull apart
the wooden crate and remove the nails without a
hammer. I find a rock that's about the size of my
fist and we use it to pound the second-hand nails
into our crutch. At least half the time we bash our
fingers instead of the nails, but eventually we get
all the pieces joined together.

Teddy picks up the assembled crutch while I
help Mr. Williams get to his feet. Teddy hands
him the crutch and Mr. Williams tucks it under
his arm before leaning his weight on it.

"Well, it's a start," he says with a wink.

Mr. Williams doesn't want to hurt our feelings
but Teddy and I can tell that we still have work
to do. We used all the nails from the crate but the
crutch is still a bit wobbly.

I think for a moment. Then I look down at the new sneakers my dad bought me last weekend. I reach down and loosen the laces until I can pull them free.

"Here," I say, holding the laces out to Teddy. "Maybe you can use these to tie the crutch together."

Teddy grins and grabs the laces from my hand. "Good idea," he says before pulling out his pocketknife.

Mr. Williams hands Teddy the crutch. Then he eases himself back onto the big rock and gives Teddy advice as he binds the joints of the crutch with my shoelaces.

"We also need something soft to go on top," I say to myself. The crutches I used last year had padding for the part that went under my arm. I head over to the tree stump where we left the food basket earlier. Most of the food is gone but the red and white checkered cloth is still there. I grab it and rush back.

Susan has finished tending to the other survivors and now she's asking Mr. Williams about his ankle. She glances at the checkered cloth in my hand but doesn't tell me to put it back. I fold the cloth in half and then wrap it around the short stick at the top of the crutch. Teddy ties it in place with the last piece of shoelace.

Susan helps Mr. Williams to stand and then watches with approval as he slips the crutch under his arm and takes a few steps on his own. This time it doesn't wobble at all.

"That's a fine crutch, boys! Just fine. Thank you," he says with misty eyes.

Mr. Williams looks at his crutch with admiration. Teddy and I beam with pride. It feels good knowing we made something that will help such a nice man.

7.

A little girl comes up and tugs at Teddy's hand. He smiles like he knows her and follows the girl to the other side of the clearing.

Susan pats her leather satchel and says, "I think we've done all we can do for today. We'll be back to check on you tomorrow, Mr. Williams. Unless you run away on your new crutch!"

Mr. Williams chuckles as he leans his crutch against the rock. Then he sits down once more, sighs, and says, "My running days are over, child."

"What about Africa?" I ask.

Mr. Williams shakes his head and holds a hand up in the air like he's about to testify in court. "'The spirit is willing, but the flesh is weak'..."

"Nonsense!" Susan exclaims in her most cheerful voice. "We'll have you up and about in no time."

Susan turns to me. "Speaking of time, we should head back. I'll gather the basket and find Teddy. We'll wait for you by the road."

I nod and wonder how Susan knew I wanted to talk to Mr. Williams a little bit longer. I'm not ready to say goodbye but I don't really have anything else to say. Mr. Williams doesn't seem to mind the silence between us. I watch as he pulls a faded blue kerchief from his pants pocket. The four corners have been tied in a knot, which Mr.

Williams' shaky fingers can't undo.

"Need some help?" I ask.

Mr. Williams nods and tosses the knotted kerchief to me. "That's for you, son. To thank you for your kindness."

"You don't have to give me anything," I say. But then I start to wonder if Mr. Williams has given me something precious like a gold ring or some rare coins. If I ever get back to my own century, a gift like that might be worth a lot of money!

I'm so excited that my fingers start to shake, too, and it takes me a while to undo the knot. I carefully open the kerchief and gasp. In the middle of the cloth square is—a pile of seeds.

I try hard not to show my disappointment. "Are they magic?" I ask hopefully.

Mr. Williams smiles at me but his eyes look sad.

"I'm afraid not, son. But those are no ordinary seeds. I brought them with me when I caught that freedom train out of Virginny. My dear old granny taught me how to grow tomatoes when I was just a boy. Never knew my mama but Granny woke me up each morning, and she was there waiting for me when I came home from the fields each night. She fed me, kept me clean, and taught me to fear the Lord. I couldn't take her with me when I left, but she gave me a kerchief just like the one I'm giving you now. Those seeds come a long way, son. And who knows—maybe some of 'em came from Africa with my granny."

I fold up the kerchief and try to give it back to Mr. Williams. "I can't take your seeds, sir."

"Why not?" he asks in a voice that sounds like he might be offended. "Those ruffians have probably trampled every living thing in my garden, but with these seeds we can start over. I don't have much, but these here seeds mean the world to me."

"That's why I can't accept them," I explain. "They're too important, too valuable. Like an heirloom."

Mr. Williams nods his head slowly. "I see what you mean. The thing is, son, I don't have nobody else to leave 'em with. And they got to be passed on. You just find them a good home. They got good soil here in Weeksville?"

"Yes, sir." I think for a moment. Then I shake half the seeds into the palm of my hand and pass the kerchief back to Mr. Williams. "You plant some in Africa and I'll plant some in Weeksville."

The old man smiles and ties up the kerchief before slipping the seeds back into his pocket.

"Alright then. Just dig a hole, drop 'em in, and give 'em a little water now and then. That ain't too hard now, is it?"

I smile and shake my head. "My mom's a good

gardener," I tell Mr. Williams. "She'll know what to do."

"You watch your mama and learn from her all you can," he says. "Then you go ahead and teach somebody else how to grow things, too. There's no greater gift, son. That kind of learning stays with you always."

I want to give Mr. Williams a hug but instead I offer him my hand. He gives it a firm shake and then pulls me close for a squeeze.

"Take care of yourself, sir," I say despite the tickle in my throat.

"You do the same, son," Mr. Williams replies with a smile.

Cradling my seeds in my hand, I head out of the woods to meet Susan and Teddy. But when I reach the edge of the woods, I see Susan standing alone by the road. She looks impatient so I turn back to see if I can find Teddy.

I spot him in a corner of the clearing. He's kneeling next to the little girl who led him away earlier. I don't have to hear what they're saying to know that Teddy is teaching the girl how to play marbles. I go up to them and clear my throat once or twice. Teddy looks up and smiles sheepishly.

"Susan's waiting for us," I remind him.

Teddy nods at me before turning to the girl. "Think you can remember all the rules I taught you?"

She nods eagerly and smiles up at Teddy. He gives her an awkward pat on the head and then Teddy reaches into his pocket and pulls out a fistful of marbles. He picks out a brilliant blue one, shoves it back in his pocket, and then pours the rest of his hard-won marbles into her cupped palms. "Share them with the others, okay?"

The girl nods before rushing off to show Teddy's gift to her friends.

"Is she any good at marbles?" I ask as we head out of the woods.

Teddy sees Susan by the road and waves. "Pretty good—*for a girl*," he says with a smirk.

I give Teddy a playful shove. "Maybe one day *she* will be the Marbles Champion of the World!"

Teddy laughs and we hurry to catch up with Susan who has already started walking up the hill.

8.

"What have you got there?" asks Susan.

I show her the seeds and Susan immediately pulls the frilly handkerchief from her sleeve. "You can't carry them like that. Wrap them up and put them in your pocket."

I accept Susan's hankie and make a little bundle by tying the four corners together. Grandpa's hat is still in my back pocket so I slip the seeds in the front pocket of my cargo shorts. I thank Susan and for a long while we walk along the dirt road in silence.

Teddy offers to carry the basket so Susan hands it to him. After a minute or two, Teddy starts tossing the empty basket up into the air and rushing ahead to catch it before it hits the ground. I wait for Susan to say something but she no longer seems to be in the mood to criticize Teddy. In fact, she looks sort of amused.

"What will happen to all those people?" I ask finally.

Susan glances at me and takes a deep breath before answering. "Well, this Sunday we'll take up a collection in church, and folks are already donating whatever they can spare. There's plenty of food to go around since we grow just about everything we eat here in Weeksville."

I think about that for a moment as I look at the

open fields and modest houses on either side of the dirt road. Then I say, "This seems like a good place for colored people to live. You're close to the city but far enough away to be—"

"Self-sufficient," Susan says with a proud lift of her chin.

"And safe," I add. "Will the survivors stay here in Weeksville?"

"Some may decide to stay, and some will leave once they find relatives or friends elsewhere who can take them in. I suspect many will be too frightened to go back into Manhattan. And I don't blame them," Susan says with a sigh. "Some have nothing left to call home."

Teddy's basket-tossing game is leading him farther and farther away from us. Susan and I watch as he disappears over the top of a hill that we haven't even started to climb. The midday sun beats down on us without mercy.

I pull my grandfather's hat from my back pocket and consider putting it on. Then I think about that little boy in the woods with the bandage on his head. I wonder whether my mom is worried about me. I rub my eyes with the back of my hand and wonder if Susan can tell that I'm wiping away sweat *and* a couple of tears.

"What will happen to the kids who have lost their parents?" I ask. "And what about the old folks? They shouldn't be sleeping on the ground like that."

Susan puts her hand on my shoulder and gives it a squeeze. "It's just for now, Dayshaun, not forever. Our people will weather this storm just as we've weathered all the others. When the riots end, no one will be left to fend for himself— least of all the children and elders. In time they'll rebuild the Colored Orphan Asylum in Manhattan, but we really need our own orphanage here in Brooklyn—and a home for the aged."

Susan presses her lips together and stares into the distance at something I can't see. "One day…"

The determined look on her face tells me that Susan has big plans for the future. She won't stop once she becomes a doctor. Not when the people in her community need so much more.

I finally decide to put on Grandpa's hat. If I don't, I'll get sunstroke before we get back to… where? I stop walking when I realize that I don't know where we're heading. I met Susan and Teddy at their neighbor's house. Will one of my new friends take me home? My stomach growls loudly, reminding me that I haven't eaten since breakfast in that other Brooklyn.

I put on the grubby old hat and start walking

again. Somehow Susan has gotten much farther ahead of me so I jog a little to catch up. But the faster I run, the farther away she gets. I finally stop running and put my hands on my knees. I'm panting pretty hard but I manage to take a deep breath and yell, "SUSAN!"

She stops for a moment and turns her head in my direction, but she doesn't seem to see me waving at her. After a moment she keeps on walking and soon she, too, has disappeared over the top of the hill.

I suddenly feel very alone. Just as panic starts to set in, the ground beneath my feet shudders and everything starts going topsy-turvy. I crouch down close to the dirt road so that I don't lose my balance and topple over. I think I'm about to travel through time again. But will I go home or farther back in time? I close my eyes and hear my dad's voice: *You can't live in the past, Dayshaun.* I really hope I go forward this time!

I don't open my eyes until it feels like the world has stopped spinning. I snatch Grandpa's hat off my head and find myself in a dark, closed-in space. When my eyes get used to the darkness, I notice a thin line of light at my feet. There's a door in front of me! I push it open and hear,

"Dayshaun? What on earth are you doing in there?"

The sound of my mother's voice makes my heart soar. I step into the bright sunlight and smile so hard that my face starts to hurt. Then I look around and realize I'm standing in the doorway of the fake privy behind the historic houses. I'm back at Weeksville Heritage Center! My mom has a quizzical look on her face but then she just laughs and waves me over.

"You remember our beekeeper Mr. Danvers, right? We were just talking about our first harvest. We have plenty of fresh vegetables to sell at the Farmer's Market on Wednesday."

"Eggplant, artichokes, carrots, kale, cabbage— and at least a few jars of honey. I think we've got something for everyone," Mr. Danvers says with satisfaction.

I look around the garden and think about what Susan told me. Weeksville was self-sufficient and that meant it could take care of everyone in the community.

"Why don't we give some of the food away?" I suggest.

Mr. Danvers' face lights up. "That's a great idea, Dayshaun. I'm sure the local food bank would appreciate some donated veggies."

"Or a soup kitchen," Mom adds. Then she beams at me and tenderly cups my face with her palm. "My sweet, reluctant gardener."

I groan and brush Mom's hand aside. "I have something for you," I say before pulling Susan's handkerchief from my pocket. For the first time I notice that her initials have been stitched in one corner. I run my finger over the satiny green thread that loops into one cursive S and then another.

I smile and look up at my mom. "A friend told me to take good care of them and I said you'd show me what to do."

Mom looks intrigued. She peers into the kerchief once I undo the knot and says, "Those are tomato seeds!"

"Yep. Can we plant them here at Weeksville?" I ask.

"Sure," Mom says. "Where did you say you got them?"

I think about Mr. Williams with his long, white beard. I hope the crutch Teddy and I built helped him to keep on moving. Maybe he even got to see Africa.

I realize that my mom is still waiting for me to answer her question. "These seeds are from an old friend," I tell her, knowing she'll probably think I mean Carlos or Tariq. I can't *wait* to tell them about my time-travel adventure!

"Well, I'm glad you're finally taking an interest in gardening," Mom says with a smile.

I slip my arm around my mom's waist and give her a squeeze. "Like you always say, Mom. We've got soil in our blood!"

THE END

Discussion Guide

1. Dayshaun doesn't share his mother's excitement about heirloom seeds until he receives some as a gift from Mr. Williams. What foods do we eat today that our ancestors ate in the past?

2. Find Liberia on a map. The African Civilization Society sent African Americans to Liberia and had its headquarters in Weeksville. Why did some people believe African Americans belonged in Africa? Where do you think YOU belong? Why?

3. Susan Smith did attend medical school and she went on to become the first African American woman doctor in New York State. Find out

more about Susan McKinney Steward's life and make a list of her achievements.

4. What is a "food desert?" Where do you find fresh food in your neighborhood? If you could design your own garden, what would you grow and how would you share your crops with your community?

5. What caused the riots in New York City and Brooklyn in 1834 and 1862? Imagine that Teddy and Susan traveled through time with Dayshaun. How has Brooklyn changed since 1863? Why do we need a Black Lives Matter movement today?

About the Author

Zetta Elliott is the award-winning author of over a dozen books for young readers. She served as the inaugural writer-in-residence at Weeksville Heritage Center in 2015. She lives in Brooklyn and loves magic, gardens, and the power that comes from knowing one's history.

Learn more at zettaelliott.com

About the Illustrator

Alex Portal currently lives in Lead, South Dakota with his wife Rachel and their cat Tiberius. He has a love of all things cartoon, and has never actually grown up.

Learn more at
http://portholeproductions.deviantart.com/gallery/

Also from Rosetta Press

$ 7.00

Best friends Carlos and Tariq love their block, but Barkley Street has started to change. The playground has been taken over by older boys, which leaves Carlos and Tariq with no place to call their own. They decide to turn the yard of an abandoned brownstone into their secret hang-out spot. Carlos and Tariq soon discover, however, that the overgrown yard is already occupied by an ancient phoenix! When the Pythons try to claim the yard for their gang, the magical bird gives the friends the courage to make a stand against the bullies who threaten to ruin their beloved neighborhood.

Learn more at www.zettaelliott.com

CPSIA information can be obtained at www.ICGtesting.com
Printed in the USA
LVOW08s0747310316

481505LV00008B/164/P